DISNEY

HIGH SCHOOL MUSICAL

STORIES FROM EAST HIGH #5

BROADWAY DREAMS

By N. B. Grace

Based on the Disney Channel Original Movie
"High School Musical", written by Peter Barsocchini

Disney PRESS

New York

Printed in the United States of America

First Edition
1 3 5 7 9 10 8 6 4 2

Library of Congress Catalog Card Number: 2007924561
ISBN-13: 978-1-4231-0623-4
ISBN-10: 1-4231-0623-7

For more Disney Press fun, visit www.disneybooks.com
Visit DisneyChannel.com

CHAPTER ONE

"**S**tudents! Settle down! Settle, please!" Ms. Darbus, the drama teacher, tried to quiet the room. Everyone who was going on the big senior class trip—this year it was to New York City!—had gathered, and she could barely be heard over the din. Ms. Darbus clapped her hands and yelled again, "I need quiet, please!"

But the noise continued—until Coach Bolton stepped to the front of the classroom, put two fingers in his mouth, and let out an ear-piercing whistle.

1

Instantly, the room went silent. "That's better," he said. "Now, I know you are all excited about going to the Big Apple, but let me make one thing perfectly clear: Ms. Darbus and I are your chaperones on this trip, which means we are responsible for your safety and well-being, which means that when one of us says to settle down, you had better settle! Understood?"

Everyone nodded meekly.

"Excellent. Ms. Darbus, you have the floor."

"Oh, well . . . thank you, Coach Bolton," the drama teacher said.

She smiled graciously and stepped to the front of the classroom (or, as she preferred to think, center stage). "Indeed, we are about to embark upon a grand journey together, an adventure that none of us will ever forget, a trip that will live on in our memories forever—"

Chad Danforth grinned at his buddy Troy Bolton, then pretended to snore.

"And that's not all! I have some very exciting news!" she continued, pointedly ignoring him.

After a long pause to make sure everyone's attention was where it should be—on her—she went on. "All of you have heard of *Last Bell!*, I hope?"

Most of the students looked puzzled, but Ryan Evans's hand shot into the air. "Yes, of course!" he cried out. "It's one of the most successful Broadway musicals of the last five years!"

"Oh, how could I have missed that?" Chad asked, rolling his eyes.

"It's set in a high school just like this one," Ryan went on. "I know all the songs by heart!" He got a faraway look in his eyes and added dreamily, "Sometimes I imagine what it would be like to appear on Broadway in a show like that. I could do it, I know I could—"

"And now you may have your chance," Ms. Darbus said.

That caught the attention of Ryan's sister, Sharpay Evans. Her head whipped around. "What?"

Ms. Darbus beamed at her. "Yes! The producers

have decided to hold open auditions for teenagers around the country! They'll choose a new cast that will perform the musical—on Broadway!—for one night only as a promotional event!"

Sharpay gasped. "This is it!" she said to Ryan. "Our destiny, our fate, our *future* has arrived!" She paused, then added, *"Finally."*

"Now, before you get too excited . . ." Ms. Darbus held up a cautionary hand. "Hundreds of other high school students will also be auditioning. The competition will be fierce!" She relaxed enough to beam at Sharpay and Ryan. "Although I'm sure that East High students are among the most talented and well-prepared in the country!"

Sharpay beamed back, knowing that when Ms. Darbus said "East High students," she really meant her, Sharpay, the best actress that East High had seen in . . . well, forever.

Oh, and she meant Ryan, too, of course.

Sharpay's hand shot up into the air. "Ms.

Darbus, what will the producers want us to do for our auditions? Should we prepare a monologue, or a dance routine, or a song, or maybe all three? And what about costumes? I know we're each allowed to bring just one suitcase on this trip, but surely those of us who are going to bring glory and renown to East High should be given an extra luggage allowance? Oh, and what about head shots and personal makeup cases and—"

"Somebody should call and warn the producers," Chad muttered to his buddies Troy, Zeke Baylor, and Jason Cross. "They may want to start planning their escape route now."

Unfortunately, his voice wasn't quite low enough.

"Thorough preparation is the sign of a true professional!" Sharpay snapped at him. "Not that I would expect *you* to know anything about being a pro!"

"That's not true," Zeke said.

Chad grinned at him. "Thanks, buddy—"

"Chad is a pro at eating. He can finish off

five hamburgers in fifteen minutes!" Zeke finished. Chad shoved him, and Zeke started laughing. Ms. Darbus just rolled her eyes. If only she were chaperoning serious, dedicated students like Sharpay and Ryan, instead of all these . . . *basketball* players!

Coach Bolton had had enough run-ins with Ms. Darbus in the past to recognize the warning signs of a full-scale snit. "Okay, enough with the chatter," he said hastily. "Let's go over the rules of the road again. We're meeting tomorrow at the airport at 6 a.m. Everyone gets to bring one suitcase—*one*, Sharpay, I don't care how many costumes you have!—and everyone is going to have to report in twice a day while we're in New York. Also, Principal Matsui wanted me to remind you that—" He glanced down at a paper he was holding. "'—this trip is supposed to be educational, so you should focus on visiting sites of historical and cultural importance.' Is that absolutely clear?"

Everyone nodded solemnly, but their eyes

were sparkling with excitement. They were going to New York City! With their best friends! What could be better?

The bell rang and they all burst into the hall, headed for their homerooms.

"This is going to be a blast," Troy said to Gabriella Montez. "What's the first thing you want to do in New York?"

"I have to go with Taylor to the television studio in the afternoon," Gabriella reminded him.

His face fell. "Oh. Right. The *College Quizmaster* show. I forgot."

"Man, I can't believe you guys actually made it to the finals!" Chad exclaimed.

"Well, we didn't have much competition," Taylor McKessie said complacently. "Even in that last round, Gabriella and I outscored the second place team by fifty points."

"You guys are awesome," Zeke said. "Serious brainiacs. Remind me to call you for tutoring when finals roll around."

Chad shook his head in mock sadness. "Too

bad you'll have to study the whole time you're in New York, and Sharpay and Ryan are going to be rehearsing the whole time. Man, I'm glad that I won't have anything to do on this trip but enjoy myself!"

"Seriously," Jason agreed. He flipped open the guidebook that he'd been carrying everywhere for the last month. "What should we do first, the Statue of Liberty or the Metropolitan Museum of Art?"

Chad looked at him as if he'd grown an extra head. "Dude, there's no contest! The number one thing we gotta do is check out Madison Square Garden!"

The other boys nodded. They couldn't wait to see the arena where the New York Knicks played.

"What about Little Italy?" Zeke asked.

"Madison Square Garden," Chad said firmly. After a moment, he asked, "Why? What's in Little Italy?"

Zeke's smile lit up the hall. "I have two words for you: awesome pastries."

"Okay, you have a point," Chad conceded. "But basketball comes first. Cookies come second."

"Cannoli," Zeke corrected him. "And don't forget tiramisu!"

"What about the Bronx Zoo? It's one of the best zoos in the world." Jason had his nose buried in his guidebook again. "When are we going to fit that in?"

"After Madison Square Garden," Chad replied. "First basketball, *then* bakeries, *then* the Bronx."

"Okay, but my book says that Central Park is a 'must-see,'" Jason insisted. "So we must see that, too. . . ."

As the three boys and Taylor walked down the hall to their next class, still arguing about their itinerary, Troy and Gabriella looked at each other and laughed.

"I think this is going to be the textbook definition of a 'whirlwind tour,'" he said.

"Yeah," she agreed, looking wistful. "I just

hope I get to do some fun stuff with you guys."

"You're only going to be on the quiz show for a few hours on Monday, right?" Troy asked. "That leaves plenty of time for, oh, I don't know. A stroll through Central Park? With, maybe, pretzels for two?"

Hanging out with Troy was always fun, but hanging out in New York . . .

Gabriella smiled at the thought, but then shook her head. "If we win the first round on Monday—"

"Which you will!" he said loyally.

"—then we'll have to go back to film again on Tuesday. And if we win on Tuesday—"

"Oh, right." Troy looked glum. "The finals are on Wednesday. And then we fly home the next day." He hesitated, then admitted, "I know this quiz show is a big deal and everything, but I wish we were going to have more time together."

"Taylor and I may not make it past the first round," Gabriella pointed out. "In which case we'll have plenty of time. . . ."

"Hey, you can't think like that," Troy said. "You gotta think like a winner! You guys are unbeatable!"

"I hope so. The grand prize is a college scholarship for each person on the winning team," she said. "It would help my mom a lot if I could win that."

"You've got a great shot," he reassured her. "And don't worry. After all, New York is the city that never sleeps, right? There will be lots of time to have some fun!"

CHAPTER TWO

The Wildcats were in New York City! After arriving at their hotel, they checked in and regrouped in the lobby. Coach Bolton automatically counted heads as Ms. Darbus flipped through her information packet.

"Here are maps of the city," she said, handing them out to everyone. "Here's a Metrocard for each of you, so you can ride on the subway or the bus. Don't forget your umbrella, the forecast says it might rain. Oh, and here's an article

12

that shows a special walking tour of all the greatest theatrical sites in the city, ending, of course, in Times Square! I highly recommend that you follow the route suggested."

Chad glanced at the article and muttered to Troy, "Like I really want to check out a costume exhibit!"

Troy stifled a laugh as Ms. Darbus glared at Chad. "I, of course, will be with Sharpay and Ryan all day at the Palace Theater, where the auditions for *Last Bell!* are being held," she said grandly. "It will undoubtedly be the most thrilling experience of all of our lives! But I'm sure the rest of you can find something equally . . . interesting to do."

Coach Bolton hid a smile at her dubious tone. He knew that Ms. Darbus couldn't imagine that anything—a world-famous art museum, a visit to Ellis Island, or a tour of the Statue of Liberty—would compare to being in a theater. Any theater, let alone a *Broadway* theater.

"All right, guys!" He clapped his hands

together as Ms. Darbus headed out the door with Sharpay and Ryan. "I want everyone to tell me your plans for the day, then I want to check that everyone's cell phone is working in case we need to get in touch with you, okay?"

"Okay!" everyone answered in chorus. They were practically jumping out of their skins with excitement. After all, who knew what adventures waited for them on the streets of New York?

Sharpay stopped dead in the middle of the street and stared up at the lights that spelled out the words: PALACE THEATER. She was completely oblivious to the screeching brakes, angry honks, and loud yells for her to "Get outta the street, already!"

"Look at that," she murmured dreamily to Ryan. "We've finally made it to Broadway!"

"Um, I'm not sure we're going to make it to tomorrow unless you move out of the traffic flow," he said, jumping as a car swerved inches away from his left elbow. "Come on!"

He grabbed her arm and hustled her over to the sidewalk. There, Ms. Darbus was reading through the instructions that had been sent to all the musical-theater hopefuls who were auditioning for *Last Bell!*

"We're supposed to go in by the stage door," she said. "It should be right around the corner...."

They followed her to an unmarked gray door and waited as she knocked.

A moment later, a heavyset man with thinning black hair opened the door. "Yeah?" he barked.

"Hi!" Sharpay gave him a big smile and fluttered her fingers at him. "We're here for the auditions!"

"Yeah, I figured as much," he said, unimpressed. He called over his shoulder. "Hey, Tim! We got two more kids here! See if you can find a place for them." He turned back to them. "Come on in, follow me, and don't touch a thing!" They nodded and followed him through the door and down a dingy hallway.

"It sounds like there are a lot of people here to audition," Ryan whispered to Ms. Darbus.

"Not to worry, Ryan, not to worry," she said, waving one hand airily. "After all, you and Sharpay are two of the brightest stars to come out of the East High drama department in years!"

"That's so true!" Sharpay agreed, preening a little bit. As the stage manager ushered them through yet another door, she added, "We shouldn't be worried about a little—"

Sharpay and Ryan stopped in shock as they walked into the auditorium.

"—competition," Sharpay finished quietly.

Ryan couldn't breathe. There were hundreds of teenagers, all staring back at them!

"Ahhh." He tried to say something, but his vocal cords didn't seem to be working.

"Breathe," Ms. Darbus's voice said in his ear. "Remember, you were the Star Dazzle award winner at the Lava Springs Country Club talent show!"

His eyes widened. "That's right, I was!"

"And you have been studying with *me* for four years," she went on.

He began to smile. "That's right, I have been!"

"And furthermore—"

"Yes, yes, Ryan's very good, but what about *me*?" Sharpay interrupted.

Ms. Darbus leaned closer to whisper to her. "And *you* have appeared in seventeen theatrical productions at East High, played the lead in the fall play and spring musical, and have been studying acting, tap, ballet, modern dance, singing, stage movement, elocution, stage combat, and mime for years."

That did the trick. Sharpay stood up straighter, a little color came back into her cheeks, and she looked at the rows and rows of other hopefuls with renewed self-confidence.

"You're absolutely right, Ms. Darbus," she said. "And all of my hard work has been leading up to this moment! I will not fail!"

"That's the spirit!" Ms. Darbus nodded in approval. "Now, let's get a seat. . . ."

* * *

A few minutes later, they were settled in the third row. Sharpay was sitting next to a girl of about her own age with long red hair, big blue eyes, and an air of complete self-confidence. She gave Sharpay a measuring glance, then granted her a smile.

It was, Sharpay couldn't help but notice, a dazzling smile.

"Hey, there," the girl said in a charming Southern drawl. "How are y'all doing? My name's Anneclaire Littlefield. I'm from South Carolina."

"Sharpay Evans, from Albuquerque. This is my brother, Ryan, and our drama teacher, Ms. Darbus." As she made the introductions, Sharpay glanced down at the folder that Anneclaire was holding. On the front, in bold letters, was written: RÉSUMÉ, HEAD SHOT, NEWS CLIPPINGS, AWARDS, ETC. The folder was more than an inch thick.

"I'm *so* pleased to meet you!" Anneclaire

followed Sharpay's gaze. She looked back up and gave a little laugh. "I thought the producers might like to read a little bit about what I've done. I mean, I'm sure all these other people—" Her gaze swept the auditorium disdainfully. "—are capable of handling the background roles, but the director will need someone with lots of stage experience to take on the lead. Fortunately, I've appeared in twenty productions at my high school, I had the lead role in seven plays, and I won Most Talented Performer three years in a row!"

"Twenty productions? Seven lead roles?" Sharpay's mind reeled. Could it be possible that this girl had a better résumé than she did?

"Yes, indeed!" Anneclaire whipped out several articles and showed them to Sharpay. The headlines read: ANNECLAIRE STEALS THE SHOW!, ANOTHER STANDING OVATION FOR ANNECLAIRE, and ANNECLAIRE—BROADWAY BOUND!

Sharpay gasped. How could she have been so foolish as to leave all of her own press clippings at home? Then she saw the triumphant glint in

Anneclaire's eyes, and her competitive spirit came surging back.

"I see you've done a lot of straight drama," she said smoothly. "Most of *my* experience has been in musical theater. Of course, that should come in quite handy for *this* audition since we're trying out for roles in a *musical*—"

"Oh, honey, you should read my program bio," Anneclaire said sweetly. "Three of my lead roles were in musicals. In fact, I choreographed the last one all by myself."

"But, but, but . . ." Ryan stammered. "*I'm* a choreographer!"

Anneclaire smiled at him kindly. "And I'm sure your dances are just real cute, darlin'! Maybe that'll help you win a spot in the chorus?"

His mouth dropped open in shock . . . and confusion. This Anneclaire person reminded him of someone, but who? He narrowed his eyes as he stared at her, racking his brain to figure out where he had met someone like her before. . . .

Ryan's thoughts were interrupted by a portly man in a blue suit who bounded out to center stage and beamed at the audience, rubbing his hands together with glee. He was followed, more slowly, by a tall, thin man with gray hair and bad posture.

"Good afternoon!" he announced. "My name is Herbert P. Smith, the director of *Last Bell!* And this—" He pointed to the other man, who lifted his hand in weary acknowledgment. "—is Albert Lackley, our producer. We'd like to offer a very warm welcome to all of you who have traveled so far to take part in our open auditions! We're very excited about the special promotional performance of our hit musical and the chance to find new, undiscovered talent. Unfortunately, we can only cast some of you in the show, but I hope the audition experience will be rewarding and educational for all of you."

A buzz ran through the auditorium as everyone glanced around the room, wondering who would be good enough to make the cut.

"I'm sure it will be educational for *some* people," Sharpay whispered to Ryan. "After all, press clippings don't win auditions!"

"And your press clippings are probably much better than hers anyway," her brother said loyally. Then a puzzled frown creased his forehead. "Why would she think my dances were 'cute'?"

Mr. Smith went on to explain that the audition process would take place in three stages. For the first part, everyone would sing a song of their own choosing. If they were asked back, they would be taught a simple dance routine to perform. And if they were asked back again, they would be given a short scene to read in order to show off their acting ability.

"Easy as pie," Anneclaire murmured.

"Yes," Sharpay said tightly. "I'm *so* looking forward to it! Especially since I won last year's holiday talent show with the song I'm going to sing!"

But when Sharpay's name was called, she walked to the center of the stage feeling a very unfamiliar sensation—nervousness. She stood for a moment, blinking in the spotlight. That bright circle of light had always seemed so warm and friendly in the past, but now it felt harsh and unforgiving.

"Um, my name is Sharpay Evans—" she began. She was shocked to hear herself. Her voice came out in a thin little whisper.

"Speak up, dear!" Mr. Smith called out. "You'll have to project a bit more than that in a Broadway theater!"

He was trying to tell *her* about projecting? Sharpay discovered that a little righteous indignation is good for the nerves. She immediately stood a little straighter, lifted her chin a defiant half-inch and said, clearly and distinctly, "My name is Sharpay Evans, and I'm going to sing 'Love Will Lift Me.'" From the corner of her eye, she could see Ryan standing backstage, waiting for his turn. He smiled encouragingly and gave her two thumbs up.

Just then, the music started and Sharpay

launched into the song. Within a few bars, she was lost in the music. Soon she was moving to the rhythm as she sang her heart out. By the end, she was giving a full-on performance that finished with a long, throbbing high C that had everyone in the theater—even the other contestants—actually applauding.

As she walked off the stage, she smiled smugly at the director and producer. Now *that*, she thought, is projecting—Broadway-style!

Her satisfaction with herself lasted through three more auditions, including Ryan's, which Sharpay judged as very good, although not quite as great as her own. He bounded off the stage, grinning with relief.

"I think I did okay, don't you?" he asked Sharpay.

"Oh, yeah, sure," his sister said absently. She couldn't really pay attention because the person who was auditioning right after Ryan was none other than Anneclaire.

Sharpay's eyes narrowed as she watched the

girl walk slowly into the spotlight and strike a pose as if she belonged there by natural right.

Which, of course, she didn't, because that was Sharpay's territory!

Then Anneclaire signaled to the pianist that she was ready, and she began to sing.

Sharpay felt as if she were going to faint. Anneclaire wasn't just good. She was *great*.

She sang an upbeat pop song that spanned almost three octaves and featured a tricky, syncopated middle section—and, to top it all off, Anneclaire had even choreographed a little dance routine to the song! She ended with a flourish, and the auditorium not only burst into applause, but some cheering as well.

Now Sharpay didn't just feel as if she were going to faint—she *knew* she was! A helpful stagehand saw her turn pale and steered her to a stool backstage.

"Oh," she moaned. "I can't believe it! I just *cannot* believe it!"

"What can't you believe?"

She looked up to see Ms. Darbus standing in front of her, her hands on her hips and a dangerous gleam in her eyes. Ryan hovered in the background, looking worried.

"I thought I'd be a shoo-in for the lead!" Sharpay whimpered. "But that . . . that girl! She's—" Sharpay hesitated. Even in her distraught state, she couldn't quite bring herself to compliment another performer. "—not too bad," she finished.

Tears welled up in her eyes as she added, "It's just like that horrible winter musical, when Gabriella wormed her way into the auditions! It's happening all over again, and it's just *not fair*!"

"Sharpay! Listen to me," Ms. Darbus snapped, a steely look in her eyes. "You are not just a very talented performer, you are *my protégé*! All you have to do is draw on the exceptional training that I have provided and you will do just fine! *Do you understand me*?"

Ms. Darbus barked out the last four words and

Sharpay, eyes wide, gulped and nodded. "Yes," she whispered. "I understand." She glanced at Ryan, who looked stunned. They had never seen this side of Ms. Darbus before.

"Good," Ms. Darbus said, nodding with satisfaction. "Now I want you to pull yourself together and start believing in yourself the way I believe in you!"

For the first time since she had heard her new rival sing, Sharpay began to smile. Ms. Darbus's delivery may have been more drill sergeant than drama teacher, but her pep talk had worked. She had managed to make Sharpay feel that she could do *anything*—even win the lead role from someone like Anneclaire Littlefield!

CHAPTER THREE

While Sharpay and Ryan were sweating out their auditions, some of the other Wildcats—Troy, Gabriella, Chad, Zeke, Jason, and Taylor—had decided to have some fun.

Well, most of them had decided to have fun. They had headed down to Greenwich Village, guidebooks in hand, to check out the area. But Gabriella and Taylor couldn't stop asking each other questions that were likely to come up on the *College Quizmaster* show.

"The father of mathematics is . . . ?" Gabriella asked Taylor.

"Archimedes!"

"Correct!" The girls gave each other a high five.

"And the British author known for his social conscience and moving portrayals of the poor in Victorian England is . . . ?" Taylor asked Gabriella.

"Charles Dickens!"

"Correct!" Taylor exclaimed.

As they gave each other another high five, Chad sighed deeply. "I don't want to spoil the fun here, but we are in New York City," he reminded them. "The Big Apple! One of the most happenin' places in the country, if not the world!"

Taylor gave him a cool look. "And your point would be?"

Chad rolled his eyes in disgust. "Quit studying for a few minutes! Look!" He flung his arm out wide to point to a pizzeria that had clearly been open for many years. Decades, in fact. "Doesn't that look like an awesome place to have lunch?"

Jason lifted his head from the guidebook he'd been studying ever since the senior class trip had been announced. "You're absolutely right, Chad," he said solemnly. "In fact, that restaurant is none other than Pietro's Pizza, established in 1903 and renowned as one of the best pizzerias in the world! The slices are world-famous and—" He leafed through his book quickly, then nodded as he found the right page. "— it's been featured in thirteen films, including the classic *Murder by Mozzarella*!"

"Really?" Troy said. "I love that movie! And I'm starving. What do you guys say . . . should we grab a slice?"

Everyone nodded enthusiastically and headed for the pizza parlor. But as they crowded through the door, Taylor murmured to Gabriella, "The Roman numeral MCMXCIX is . . ."

"1999," Gabriella whispered back.

"Correct!" They gave each other a furtive low

five, then looked up at the menu board to choose the slice they wanted to order.

"What do you say, Gabriella?" Troy said in a teasing voice. "Are you going for your favorite combo, pepperoni-and-pineapple?"

"What?" Jason looked up from his guidebook, shocked. "This is New York, man! You've gotta order a traditional slice! Look!" He flipped the book around to show him the section on New York City pizzeria history and stabbed his finger at the entry for Pietro's. "Tomato and cheese, or sausage, or margherita, but *no pineapple*!"

"You're absolutely right, Jason," Gabriella said, trying not to laugh at how earnest he was. "When in New York, you've got to eat like a New Yorker."

They all ended up ordering a simple slice with cheese and tomato sauce. After taking the first bite, Taylor looked at Jason with round eyes. "Your guidebook did not steer you wrong, my friend," she said. "This is awesome pizza!"

Jason nodded, a bit smug. "Wait till we get to

the next spot they recommend. The best hot dogs in the world!"

Tension was high in the Palace Theater as Mr. Smith took the stage once again, this time holding a piece of paper. "Ladies and gentlemen! We want to thank you from the bottom of our hearts for the effort you put into these auditions. Sadly, not everyone can go on to the next round, but those whom we would like to ask back are . . ."

He began reading off a list of names.

Sharpay had her eyes squeezed shut and her fingers crossed on both hands. "Please, please, *please*," she muttered to herself. "I'll do anything, I'll paint sets, I'll iron costumes, I'll be nice to every understudy I ever have—"

"Anneclaire Littlefield!"

Anneclaire let out a shriek of joy, right in Sharpay's ear. Sharpay closed her eyes even tighter and crossed her toes as well. . . .

"Sharpay Evans! Ryan Evans!"

"Yessss!!!" Sharpay's eyes popped open and she jumped up, high-fiving her brother and then Ms. Darbus. "I *did* it!"

"Of course you did," Ms. Darbus said calmly.

Sharpay sat down again, smiling with happy relief. And silently, she decided that any promises about painting sets, ironing costumes, or being nice to understudies were null and void, since she had muttered them under extreme duress.

Soon the director had finished reading off the callback list. "Please be here tomorrow morning at nine a.m. sharp for your dance audition," he said. "Thank you, and good night."

Sharpay, Ryan, and Ms. Darbus joined the crowd leaving the auditorium. Half of the people were bubbling with excitement, loudly chattering about what they planned to do to prepare for the next day's audition. The other half was downcast, quietly reassuring each other that they didn't care a bit about not being called back because now they'd have that much more time to go sightseeing. . . .

Sharpay grandly ignored everyone. "That wasn't so bad after all!" she said brightly. "I don't know why I got so nervous, it was ridiculous, really—"

"Hey," Anneclaire interrupted. "Y'all did pretty good in the singing audition."

"Thank you," Sharpay said coolly. With all the graciousness she could muster, she added, "Your audition was quite . . . respectable as well."

"Of course, the singing is the easiest part! Tomorrow is where I'm really going to shine!" Anneclaire continued. "My drama teacher says that it's almost impossible for her to decide what my strong point is as a performer, but that she'd have to say that my dancing is even better than my singing!"

Ryan gasped. Now he knew who this girl reminded him of! She sounded exactly like . . . Sharpay!

"I know, it's hard to believe," Anneclaire went

on, mistaking his expression for awe. "Even I was pleased with my singing today, and my biggest flaw is that I am a total perfectionist! For example, I know Mr. Smith said that we'd all have to learn a little dance for tomorrow's audition, but I just talked to him and explained that I love *Last Bell!* so much that I've spent the last two months creating an original dance for the big cafeteria number in the second act. And you know what he said? He said he'd be really interested in seeing it!"

Sharpay tried not to whimper. Why hadn't she thought of doing that?

Anneclaire leaned toward them and whispered conspiratorially, "And you know what else? He told me he thinks that the dance they've been using is getting a little tired, so he wants to see if my ideas can freshen it up a bit." She beamed at them. "Now wouldn't that be something? To have a Broadway choreography credit before I even graduate from high school?"

"Yes," Ryan said insincerely. "That would really be . . . something."

"Well, I'd better get back to the hotel and run through my routine a few times. See y'all tomorrow!"

And with a jaunty wave, she was gone.

For a long moment, Sharpay, Ryan, and Ms. Darbus stood motionless in the lobby. Then Sharpay murmured faintly, "I think I need to freshen up a bit." She headed for the restroom, closely followed by Ms. Darbus.

Ryan wandered around the lobby, looking at photos of the current cast members that were hung on the wall. He took a deep breath. Even the air in the lobby seemed filled with the vibrations of legendary performances, thrilling theatrical history, and spectacular stories of understudies who became stars. . . .

Then he sneezed. It was filled with a lot of dust, too.

After a few minutes, he realized that he had left his umbrella in the auditorium. He opened the door leading into the huge, darkened room and felt a shiver of excitement run through him. It was fantastic to be in the audience watching a show, of course, but it was even better to be in the theater when no one else was there, he thought.

In the dark and the quiet, you could imagine yourself up there on the stage.

In the dark and the quiet, you could visualize the audience focused totally on you, responding to your performance.

In the dark and the quiet, you could . . .

. . . hear the director and producer of *Last Bell!* talking about the auditions they had just witnessed.

Quickly, he ducked down behind the seats, hoping they hadn't seen him. Not that he was doing anything wrong—he was just looking for an umbrella—but he didn't want them to think he was sneaking around where he wasn't supposed to be.

"Lotta great kids up there," Mr. Smith said

to Mr. Lackley. "Too bad we can't use them all."

The producer shrugged. "That's showbiz," he said wearily as he double-checked a list. "Is there some reason we had to buy three new costumes last week? And why are we repainting the set again? Didn't we do that six months ago?"

Mr. Smith ignored these questions. After all, you couldn't stage a filet-mignon musical on a hot-dog budget. He squinted at the stage. "So I had an idea about changing the production number at the end of Act One," he said. "The cheerleader-and-basketball-player dance is getting kind of tired."

"If you say so," Mr. Lackley said, putting on reading glasses and peering at another paper that was covered with numbers. "Why are we twenty grand over budget on lights? Is someone breaking the bulbs every night?"

"Yeah, we need to spice that number up," Mr. Smith continued. "In fact, I had an absolute inspiration this morning when I was taking my shower!"

Mr. Lackley groaned. The last time the direc-tor had an inspiration in the shower it had cost millions.

"I'm thinking we should change the number completely, from top to bottom!" Mr. Smith went on. "I'm thinking we should do some kind of historical revue, you know, have the kids doing dances from the past five decades. Flashback numbers are always a big hit."

"I'm thinking it sounds expensive," the pro-ducer said gloomily. "I suppose you'd need all-new costumes?"

"A minor detail!" Mr. Smith waved a hand dismissively. "This is genius! We start with the '40s, with all the kids jitterbugging around the stage, then move to the '50s, when they're all dressed like Elvis, then the '60s, with lots of hip-pie clothes and psychedelic lights, and then the '70s—"

"I remember the '70s," Mr. Lackley interrupted. After a moment, he added, "I didn't like them."

"People will love it! No matter what age you

are, there will be something for you!" Mr. Smith was actually jumping up and down in the aisle, he was so excited. "Let's call Darien and get him to work up a section for the kids to try tomorrow in their auditions. I think the '60s 'Summer of Love' part would be fun, don't you? The kids'll really get into that. . . ."

Their voices faded as they left the auditorium. After a moment, Ryan's head popped up and he looked around warily. The coast was clear.

He trotted back up the aisle and into the lobby, where Sharpay, fully recovered, was tapping her foot impatiently.

"Where were you, Ryan?! We've been waiting forever!" she exclaimed.

"Don't worry, it was worth it," he said, smiling slyly at her. "Wait till you hear what I found out about tomorrow's auditions. . . ."

He started talking as they left the theater. It wasn't until ten minutes later, when the rain began to fall, that he realized that he had never found his umbrella.

CHAPTER FOUR

"**W**hoa!" Chad jumped back to the curb as a cab came hurtling around the corner. "Slow down, dude!"

"This is New York," Taylor said. "I think they're required by law to drive like that." She looked at Chad, who was stunned. "Are you okay?"

Chad took a deep breath. "Oh, yeah. Just taking a little break to make sure my heart is still working. Hey, where is everybody?"

They turned to see Gabriella and Troy staring in the window of a store that sold only retro lunch boxes from the '60s, and Zeke gazing at the pastries in the bakery next door. Jason was standing right in the middle of the sidewalk, reading his guidebook and completely ignoring irritated comments from the people who had to walk around him.

Taylor sighed. Greenwich Village was completely awesome, but there was so much interesting stuff to see that it had taken them almost half an hour to walk ten blocks. And they only had a few short days to tour the whole city!

She grabbed Chad and they went back to Troy and Gabriella.

"That *Lost in Space* lunch box is so cute!" Gabriella was saying. "Maybe we should go in and see what else they have."

Jason wandered up. "Hey, look, my book says that there's a park that runs along the river just a few blocks away. Maybe we should check it out, now that it's stopped raining!"

"Sounds good," Troy said.

"But I thought we were headed for the Statue of Liberty," Taylor said. "We can't visit New York and not see that. We're supposed to be checking out historical and cultural spots, remember?"

Chad motioned toward Zeke who was still in front of the bakery window. He looked as if he were lost in a dream—a particularly happy dream, judging by the glazed look in his eyes. "I think it's time to do a doughnut intervention," Chad said. "Zeke looks like he's gone into a trance."

They all laughed and walked over to Zeke.

"Come on, dude, we've got lots of ground to cover," Chad said.

"Look at those cannoli," Zeke said in a dreamy voice. "And the sfogliatelle and the pignoli and the spumenti!"

Chad looked. So did the rest of them. And within seconds, they had the same faraway look in their eyes. Then Zeke pointed to a sign in the window. "Hey, this place has been around since 1873! That means it's historical, right?"

The others nodded.

"And the desserts are all *Italian*, which means they're from *Italy*, which is another *culture*—"

"You don't have to convince us, man," Chad said. "Come on, we gotta check this place out!"

Twenty minutes later, they were on their way again, after having taste-tested a dozen different cookies they had never heard of before, but now couldn't wait to have again. Zeke had spent the entire time talking to the bakery's owner, who had given him several useful tips about cream fillings and then handed him a bag with a few biscotti for the road.

"That was great!" Troy said happily as they strolled on down the street.

"Yeah, but if I lived here, I'd gain five pounds in a week," Gabriella said. "The food is just too good."

"You'd work it off walking around," Chad said.

"And jumping out of the way of cabs," Taylor added dryly.

Just then, Troy caught sight of something that immediately made him feel at home: a basketball court. "Hey, guys, check this out," he said, heading across the street.

The court was really a playground, surrounded on all four sides by a tall chain-link fence. It was about half the size of a regular basketball court. A few people were standing by the fence and checking out the action inside as six guys played a fast and furious game of three-on-three.

The Wildcats joined the spectators to watch. "Man, those guys are good!" Troy said in awe.

"No lie," Chad agreed as one of the players raced down the court and slam-dunked the ball through the bent metal rim.

Jason actually closed his guidebook and put it in his backpack so that he could pay more attention to the game. Zeke nibbled a biscotti as he watched one of the players fake out another one with a sweet move that he vowed to try himself the next time he was on the court.

Soon there was a break in the action. "I'm done. Gotta be at work in an hour," one of the players said.

"I'm outta here, too," another guy said.

As they walked off the court, one of the remaining players said to his friends, "Well, I guess that's it for today—"

"Hey, you guys want a little more competition?" Chad called out.

Troy gave him a startled look. What was Chad *doing*? Sure, the game looked like fun, but those guys were big and strong and *really* good. . . .

Two of the players looked at each other and grinned, then came over to the fence. "You boys play ball?"

"You bet!" Jason said confidently. "In fact, last year we won—"

"—a few games here and there," Troy interrupted quickly. He knew Jason didn't mean to brag about winning the championship—he was

46

just proud of what they'd done together—but it might not come off that way to these strangers.

"So," said one of the players, "you want a quick pickup game?"

The other Wildcats looked to Troy to see what he would say. He hesitated. They hadn't come to New York City to play ball, after all, and his dad had reminded them all that the trip was supposed to be educational.

"I don't know," the other player said to his friend. "Maybe we should ask them to get a note from their mommas. . . ."

That did it.

"You're on," Troy said. After all, he reasoned, they would probably learn a little something about basketball from these guys, which would make the experience educational, right?

Chad, Zeke, and Jason broke into wide grins as they hurried through the gate to start the game.

Thirty minutes later, the Wildcats were wondering what, exactly, they had gotten themselves into.

The guys they were playing against were named Terence, Reggie, Max, and Bongo. Bongo wasn't really tall, but he could hit one three-pointer after another. Terence got unbelievable air when he jumped; he was always taking passes up the middle and jumping what seemed like three feet above everyone's heads to hit his shots. Max was a master at stealing the ball. And Reggie—Reggie was just an immovable object. He'd stand under the basket like a brick wall and the Wildcats couldn't get position on him, no matter how hard they tried. He got every rebound and turned it into a basket. All four of them were extremely fast, excellent at blocking shots, and played the whole game above the rim, slam-dunking the ball over and over.

"Okay," Troy said to the other Wildcats. "Let's focus on the fundamentals. We know we're good at that."

"Yeah!" Chad exclaimed. Despite everything, he still had some swagger left. "Let's show 'em how it's done!"

But when they took the court again, Chad tried setting a pick—and the other team was so fast that another defender moved in and Troy couldn't get an open shot. Max stole the ball and passed it to Bongo, who hit yet another three-pointer. Then Reggie grabbed the inbound pass and made another basket. A few moments later, Chad managed to get his hands on the ball, but Terence stole it and lofted it from somewhere in the stratosphere . . . and that's when the Wildcats started falling apart.

They were so flustered by the kind of game they were in—and the fact that they couldn't seem to counter anything these guys threw at them—that they started taking wild shots, getting more discouraged by the minute.

Finally, Troy managed to twist away from a defender. He jumped and launched a shot. To his surprise, it hit the backboard and dropped in.

Chad gave him a high five and Zeke called out, "Great shot!" But Troy had to face the facts. That was one basket for the Wildcats—

and about a hundred for their opponents.

"Not bad," Terence said with a friendly grin.

"Yeah, sometimes luck's as good as talent," Reggie added, not quite as friendly.

"Come on, man, the boys here did their best," Terence said.

Troy could see Chad start to react to that, and he stepped in hastily. "Thanks for the game," he said. "We learned a lot."

"I bet you did," Reggie snickered. "Come back any time. We hold class here every afternoon."

"Hey, you know we'll be back," Chad said. "And we'll be bringing our A-game, too!"

"You do that." Terence chuckled.

"Yeah, you bring your A-game . . . as soon as you find it," Reggie said. Then, as they walked through the gate, Reggie called after them, "Welcome to the Cage, boys!"

"Well, that was . . . instructional," Troy said. The Wildcats, including Gabriella and Taylor, were walking down the street. The boys were still in shock and trying to figure out what had gone wrong.

"I can't believe it! Those guys didn't look much older than us!" Chad fumed. He stopped in mid-stride as a thought struck him. "Do you think maybe they were practicing for the NBA draft or something?"

"At a cramped little place like that?" Zeke said. "Not likely."

Gabriella decided it was time to focus on the positive. "I thought you guys looked pretty good, considering you hadn't warmed up, and you weren't used to playing on such a small court, and—"

"And we didn't actually let them steal the ball more than, oh, thirty times," Chad interrupted.

Troy was thinking. "Yeah, we can make all the excuses we want, but the fact is . . . we were schooled."

The other boys looked depressed to hear their captain state the obvious. Then Troy cracked a tiny smile and said, "But that doesn't mean we can't come back, does it?"

"Come back here?" Jason had his guidebook open again. "But I've circled twelve more spots of interest, including the tavern where George Washington gave his farewell speech to the troops. . . ."

"And I promise we'll get to at least five of those historic sites," Troy said. Then, with a look of determination, he added, "But I also promise that those guys have not heard the last of us. What do you guys say?"

"I say, yes, we're coming back, and yes, we're going to beat those dudes!" Chad yelled. "What team?"

"Wildcats!" they all yelled in response.

"*What team?*"

"WILDCATS!!!"

Gabriella looked around, hoping no one was staring at them, doing cheers in the middle of the street. Then she remembered. This was New York. No one even noticed.

CHAPTER FIVE

After a little more discussion, the Wildcats realized that everyone wanted to do different things. So they agreed to split up for the rest of the afternoon, then meet that night for dinner. Chad and Zeke headed uptown to check out Central Park. Jason was determined to take a tourist bus around the city and go to the top of the Empire State Building. Taylor wanted to explore a museum devoted to Tibetan art. And Troy and Gabriella . . . well, they just wanted to walk around the city and look at everything. As long as they were together, they knew they'd have fun.

They started to explore Greenwich Village. Unlike the area around their hotel, where the streets were laid out in an easy-to-understand grid, the streets in the Village ran at all kinds of crazy angles. Within five minutes, they were poring over their map; within seven minutes, they realized they were totally lost; and within ten minutes they decided to forget the map and just wander around.

For the next hour, they poked their heads into record stores that sold thousands of old-school records—the kind you had to put on a turntable. They browsed through comics stores and a used bookstore that had eighteen miles of books. They watched jugglers, street musicians, and some very serious chess players in Washington Square Park. And finally, they were tired enough to sit down at an outdoor café and have a soda.

"This is so great!" Gabriella exclaimed as she watched the people walking by. "I almost wish Taylor and I hadn't made the *College Quizmaster* finals, so we'd have more time to hang out."

"Yeah," Troy said. "That would be fun."

She glanced over at him. He seemed lost in thought; he wasn't even looking at the street scene. Instead, he was sipping his soda and frowning down at the tablecloth.

"Is something wrong? You seem a little . . . preoccupied," she said.

"What?" He looked up and seemed to refocus his eyes. "Oh, sorry. I just keep thinking about that pickup game. Maybe if I had better moves, we would have . . . well, not won, but maybe not have embarrassed ourselves."

"Come on, Troy," Gabriella said. "You guys weren't embarrassing. You were just—"

"Outplayed." He tried to smile at her, but he was still glum.

"Hmm." She sat silently for a few minutes, sipping her soda. Then she asked, "So who would you say is the best basketball player of all time?"

"Why?" he asked, puzzled.

"Well, I have a feeling you're going to be thinking about basketball for the rest of the afternoon, even if you try not to," she teased him. "I thought we might as well go with it."

He grinned. "Yeah, you're right," he admitted. "It's going to be hard to shake off that game."

"And I'd rather not think about going on *College Quizmaster* tomorrow," she added. "So tell me about the all-time best player."

"Okay," he said readily. "No question, it was Michael Jordan. He led the Chicago Bulls to six championships in the '90s. He's also a great all-around athlete. You know, he's an excellent golfer." He said that with such a sense of satisfaction that Gabriella had to laugh. Troy was also on the East High golf team when he wasn't playing basketball. "*And* he even quit basketball and played minor-league baseball for a season in 1994."

"Really?" she said. "I didn't know that. So what made him so good at basketball?"

"Well, he could do everything—shoot, steal the ball, rebound, defend . . . and he'd do whatever he had to do to win the game," Troy answered. "But mostly I think he just really loved playing. In fact, he put it in his contract that he could play basketball any time he wanted in the off-season, which most NBA stars can't do. It was called his 'love-of-the-game' clause. Now, let me tell you about the six championships the Bulls won. . . ."

"Sharpay! Look!" Ryan had been trailing his increasingly impatient sister through the East Village for what seemed like days. And that was after undergoing the stress and strain of an audition! Just as he thought he might actually faint from exhaustion, he spotted a small store down a side street that seemed to call to him.

He hurried over and came to a halt in front of the tiny storefront.

"What is it?" Sharpay snapped. She stopped, looked around, and retraced her steps to find Ryan looking in the front window, his eyes glowing and his mouth hanging half open.

"Look," he whispered, pointing at the window.

She turned to see what had caught Ryan's attention, hoping that he hadn't been side-tracked by yet another aromatherapy store. Basil-lemon candles were all very well, but they had a mission to complete.

Then she saw the clothes displayed in the store window. Bell bottoms that flared out over platform shoes. Miniskirts paired with go-go boots and a psychedelic top. Skinny black pants with ankle boots. Jackets with beading and feathers. Colorful plastic earrings and necklaces. In other words, it was—

"Sixties Heaven," Ryan said in awe.

After a moment, Sharpay realized that he wasn't being poetic. That was actually the name of the shop, painted above the door in rounded letters. "Well, what are we waiting for?" she cried happily. "Our audition-winning costumes await us!"

They pushed through the door into a dim room that smelled like incense. Somewhere in the back of the shop, a bell rang softly, and a long-haired girl wearing granny glasses, patched jeans, and a gauze blouse emerged from the back room.

"Hey," she said in a laid-back voice. "How are you guys doing today?"

Ryan got a silly grin on his face. "We're, um, groovy."

She smiled back. "That's cool."

"Your whole store is cool," he replied. "The whole vibe is just really, um—"

"Yes, yes, yes, it's cool and groovy and ever so '60s," Sharpay said impatiently. "But we don't have time for your hippie act. We're in a hurry."

The girl raised her eyebrows, but she nodded and said crisply, "Fine. How can I help you?"

"I need a fantastic 'Summer of Love' costume," Sharpay said, "and I need it *now*."

Half an hour later, Sharpay and Ryan left Sixties Heaven carrying two bags each. Sharpay had put together an outfit (with the help of Angela, the sales clerk) that included hiphugger jeans, a silk blouse covered with orange, pink, and red swirls, oversized sunglasses, clunky sandals, and rings for every finger and both thumbs. Ryan had bought faded jeans, a leather vest and hat, and a drapey white shirt that made him feel vaguely like a pirate. He had also developed a serious crush on Angela.

"She said her mother named her Angela because she looked like an angel when she was born," he said with a sigh. "And she still does, don't you think?"

Sharpay stopped in the middle of the sidewalk and swung around to face him. "Ryan! Pull yourself together! We are going to one of the biggest auditions of our lives tomorrow and we need to be ready. Costumes show what your character looks like—"

"—but acting reveals what your character feels." He finished the sentence with her. They both knew the slogan by heart; Ms. Darbus repeated it constantly during rehearsals, especially when cast members complained about the outfits given to them by the costume department.

"Exactly! I need to *prepare*, I need to *feel* what the 'Summer of Love' was like, I need to be able to engage all my *senses* in the spirit of the '60s— and I need to do it *tonight*!" Sharpay clutched her head, the very picture of despair.

"Don't worry, sis, I've got you covered." With a smug smile, Ryan whipped out a flyer that he had picked up at Sixties Heaven. It read: "One Night Only! Experience Woodstock in Central Park! Performing: The Foggy Prunes."

Sharpay's eyes widened with delight. "Ryan! This is perfect!"

"I know." He sighed. "Just like Angela."

Sharpay rolled her eyes.

"Hey, that's who gave me the flyer," Ryan said defensively.

That evening, as the sun was setting over the Hudson River, Sharpay and Ryan went to Central Park. They walked along a road that circled a lake, along with dozens of joggers and bikers. When they got to the stage where The Foggy Prunes were performing under a canopy of trees, they saw thousands of other people there. The music started and, before long, everyone was moving and grooving to the sounds of the '60s.

"This is great!" Sharpay exclaimed, watching a man and woman dancing nearby. They were wearing clothes very similar to the ones that she and Ryan had bought, and they had some cool moves that she quickly memorized. After all, there might be a chance to do a few improvised steps tomorrow, and she wanted to be ready. "I'm going to be so much better than that Anneclaire, I just know it!"

"Of course you will," Ryan said absently.

"What's wrong with you?" Sharpay snapped. "You're not listening to a word I'm saying."

"What?" He quickly turned to look at her. His eyes seemed to come back into focus, and he put an interested look on his face. "Of course I am! You were just saying, um . . ." He hesitated. Actually, he hadn't been listening, but it wasn't hard to guess what Sharpay had been talking about. "You were saying that you're going to be great tomorrow! And you will be! Because you're the best singer, dancer, actress, and producer on the planet!"

Sharpay eyed him suspiciously—even she thought that was a tad over-the-top—but decided to accept the compliment graciously. "Well, that's true."

"But you know, even if we don't win the auditions—"

Sharpay's mouth dropped open. "Don't even think that!" she hissed.

But Ryan went on stubbornly. "Even if we

don't—which we *absolutely will*—I think it's kind of neat to be here, don't you?" He gestured toward the grassy lawn, the flowers and trees, the band, the music, and the people laughing and dancing in the mellow light of the setting sun.

"It would be kind of *neat* to make my Broadway debut, Ryan," she sniffed. "That's what I need to focus on."

But Ryan wasn't listening . . . again! Instead, he was staring past her shoulder, a now-familiar dazed look in his eyes.

"Hey, guys!"

Sharpay turned around to see Angela, still dressed in her hippie outfit, smiling at them. "I'm glad you made it to the concert," she said. "The Foggy Prunes are one of my favorite bands."

"Yeah, mine, too," Ryan said, smiling foolishly. "I mean, I never heard of them before . . . but after tonight . . . well, now they're my favorite band of all time!"

Sharpay rolled her eyes, but Angela smiled and held out her hand. "That's cool," she said. "Wanna dance?"

Ryan gulped, but managed to nod. He followed her into the crowd, where they began doing some kind of old-school dance. Now that Ryan was in his element, he looked more confident. He relaxed, began smiling, and even pulled Angela into an improvised dance movement.

As Sharpay watched, she found herself smiling, too. For a few moments, she forgot the stress and pressure of embarking on a major entertainment career and let herself just listen to the music. And as the band played on, the sun set, and the smell of hot dogs and pretzels drifted on the breeze, she had to admit, a concert in Central Park was kind of . . . neat.

CHAPTER SIX

The next morning, Gabriella and Taylor got up early. Way too early, in Taylor's opinion. But they had to get dressed, have breakfast, and get to Rockefeller Center for the taping of the game show, which started at eight a.m. sharp.

"Are you nervous?" Gabriella asked as they rode over in a cab.

"No, of course not," Taylor said. "We've been studying for months. We are totally ready, girl."

"You're right," Gabriella agreed. "We're, um, bringing our A-game, right?"

Taylor chuckled to hear Gabriella try out sports slang. "You got it."

They got out of the cab and walked to the TV studio. They stopped in front of the building for just a minute to take a photo of the famous golden statue of Prometheus, which overlooked the flags of all the countries in the world. Then they hustled through the lobby and up to the fifteenth floor, where a production assistant greeted them, took them to a room to wait, and scurried off again.

Four other teenagers were already there. Everyone awkwardly introduced themselves. There were two boys dressed in sharp suits. The dark-haired boy said his name was Chase P. Pearson; the blond boy was Sinclair Farmington.

"We're the Muskrats," Chase said. "From Connecticut."

"You didn't have far to travel then," Gabriella said, trying to make conversation.

Sinclair raised one eyebrow. "Well, you'll certainly score a lot of points on the geography section," he said snidely. Chase snickered.

Gabriella blushed and turned to the other two contestants. They were from a small town in Ohio where the team name was the Dragons. An intense girl with shoulder-length dark hair and black-framed glasses was named Winnie Barnes; her teammate, a short girl with red hair, was named Jan Stevens.

"We didn't get here until midnight last night," Jan said anxiously. "Our plane was delayed forever because of bad weather! I just hope we still do okay. . . ."

"Oh, I'm sure you will—" Gabriella started to say sympathetically, but she was cut off by Sinclair.

"That's too bad," he said, not even bothering to sound like he meant it. "Lack of sleep can really mess up focus and concentration. But it'll make a great come-from-behind story if you end up winning. More drama for the reality show segment, you know."

"What are you talking about?" Taylor frowned at him. She'd already decided that she didn't like this Sinclair or his pipsqueak partner. It would feel good to see them go down. "What reality show segment?"

At that moment, two men burst into the room. One had a TV camera perched on his shoulder; the other carried a clipboard.

"Welcome, *College Quizmaster* contestants!" the man with the clipboard cried. "I'm Bert, the producer, and this is Joe, one of our incredible cameramen. We'll be filming you all the time you're here—as you wait backstage, as you do last-minute cramming, as you have meltdowns in the halls! Every dramatic moment will be captured so that our viewing audience can really *feel* the tension of appearing on a nationally televised game show and being asked impossibly difficult questions!"

Jan and Winnie turned pale.

Sinclair and Chase smirked.

Gabriella felt her stomach lurch.

Taylor just rolled her eyes. Please. As if regular life weren't dramatic enough, she thought. These guys think they have to take it to the next level.

"Now don't feel you have to act or fake anything for the camera," Bert went on. "Just be your normal, lovely selves . . . although, if you feel like you're about to have a panic attack or burst into hysterical sobs, please give Joe the high sign. That's exactly the kind of visual that really pulls the audience in, you know what I mean? Now let's get started with some one-on-one interviews. Who'd like to go first? Chase? Excellent. Let's go next door, shall we?"

When Sharpay and Ryan swept into the Palace Theater the next day wearing their '60s costumes, every head turned to look at them with a mixture of surprise and jealousy. Mr. Smith's eyebrows rose almost to his hairline, but then he broke into a grin and came bustling over to them.

"Well, this is definitely going above and beyond the call of duty!" he exclaimed. "I didn't ask for it. I didn't expect it. But I'm impressed! Yes, very impressed, indeed!"

Sharpay tossed her head. "It's just a little something we pulled together last night."

Behind them, Ms. Darbus beamed.

Then the choreographer clapped his hands and called out, "Okay, everybody onstage! I'm going to show you the routine now. We'll spend a little time practicing it, then everyone gets paired up to do it for the auditions."

As the teens filed onto the stage, Sharpay ended up next to Anneclaire. She gave her rival an insincere smile and said, "I love your black leotard. It was so brave of you to go for the minimalist look. And your makeup is so . . . understated."

Anneclaire returned Sharpay's fake smile with one of her own. "Thanks. I believe that a *true* artist should rely on nothing but her talent. As my drama coach always says, sometimes a beautiful jewel looks best in a simple setting."

Ms. Darbus scowled as she overheard this. As far as she was concerned, the more elaborate the set and costumes and props, the better.

"I'm sure that approach worked back in your little school," Sharpay said. "But we'll see how it plays on Broadway."

"You bet we will," Anneclaire murmured.

Half an hour later, it was time for Sharpay and Ryan to perform. As usual, Ryan did a very credible job, but Sharpay went all-out: she whirled across the stage, not only performing the dance they'd just been taught, but throwing in some extra moves that she had picked up from the previous night's concert. At the end, the room burst into cheering applause that Sharpay knew was louder and longer than what had greeted Anneclaire after her singing audition.

Beaming with happiness, Sharpay and Ryan ran down the steps to sit in the audience next to Ms. Darbus. They watched as other performers took the stage, quietly trading comments about each one.

"Too stiff," Ms. Darbus commented.

"Too clumsy," Sharpay ruled.

"Forgot the steps!" Ryan shook his head in disbelief.

"Tripped in the middle!" That stunned all three of them.

Then it was Anneclaire's turn. She was teamed with a lanky boy who had to keep brushing his hair out of his eyes.

"Not a good sign," Ms. Darbus whispered. "It's hard to do your best when your partner can't see you."

"Oh, what bad luck for her." Sharpay smiled.

But then the music started and, within five bars, Sharpay's smile disappeared.

Despite her lack of costume and makeup, Anneclaire did not show any lack of talent. In fact, Sharpay had to admit, as she watched in horror, that Anneclaire's simple leotard focused more attention on the precision of her dance steps. And it didn't matter that her partner wasn't that good, because no one watched him for one second. As long as Anneclaire was onstage, every eye was on her and only her.

She finished to even wilder applause and louder cheers. She bounded down the steps and up the aisle. As she passed Sharpay, she said, "Your costume looked real cute up there, honey. And I'm sure the director was only a little bit distracted by all those beads around your neck. . . ."

"How long did the Hundred Years' War between England and France last?"

Bzzz! Taylor's hand hit the button in front of her. They weren't going to trap her with a trick question! "One hundred sixteen years," she said confidently. "From 1337 to 1453."

"Correct!" cried the host for *College Quizmaster*, a bouncy man with red hair and a blinding-white smile. "Next question: wind speed is measured by what instrument?"

Winnie hit her buzzer. "An anemometer."

"Correct! Next question—"

"Invented in 1450," she added.

The host nodded, still smiling. "Yes, thank you, but you already got points for the right answer—"

"By Leon Battista Alberti," she continued. "He was an Italian artist and architect—"

The host wasn't smiling anymore. "Yes. Thank you. No extra credit is given on *College Quizmaster* for superfluous and unrequested information. Let's all try to keep that in mind," he said tightly. "Moving on, please. Next question: when was the idea of the atom first introduced and by whom?"

Bzzz! Chase's hand hit his button. "Approximately 450 BC, by Leucippus of Miletus."

"Correct!" The host grinned at the audience. "This is the closest match-up I've ever seen on *College Quizmaster*! It's turning into a real nail-biter! Let's see if we can stump our teams with this next question, which has three parts. What was the name of the world's first postage stamp, what was on it, and when was it introduced?"

Gabriella hit her buzzer. "It was called the Penny Black, it had a portrait of Queen Victoria on it, and it was introduced in 1840," she reeled off.

The host laughed and shook his hand as if it had just been burned. "These teams are on fire today, folks! The Muskrats have 125 points, the Wildcats are right at their heels with 123 points, and the Dragons are not far behind with 119 points. Let's take a quick commercial break and come back to see who comes out on top!"

As soon as she was sure they weren't filming, Gabriella leaned over to whisper to Taylor. "Those guys are good," she said, nodding to the other teams. "Really good."

"That's okay," Taylor replied. "As long as we're better." She took a long look at Gabriella. "You're not worried, are you?"

Before Gabriella could answer, Joe swooped in with his camera. Bert was right behind him.

"So," the producer said to Gabriella and Taylor, "you're only two points behind, but you're facing tougher competition than you've ever faced before! How do you feel right now?"

Gabriella gave him a big smile. "Terrific."

"We're right where we want to be," Taylor added, her voice ringing with confidence.

"Those other teams are looking very strong, though. Sure you don't feel a little nervous? Maybe like you're about to cry?" the producer asked, a light of hope in his eyes.

"Not in the slightest," Gabriella said sternly. "This is actually a lot of fun."

As the disappointed producer went to interview Winnie and Jan, Gabriella closed her eyes for a moment and swallowed hard. *Fun* wasn't quite the right word for this experience, she thought. Actually, *terrifying* was a little closer to the mark.

CHAPTER SEVEN

The mood at dinner that night was subdued. Coach Bolton and Ms. Darbus took the Wildcats to a famous Italian restaurant, known for serving huge bowls of spaghetti that everyone could share, family style. They expected a lot of excited chatter about auditioning for a Broadway musical, appearing on a television quiz show, and seeing the sights of New York.

Instead, Sharpay was saying, "How could that girl upstage me—*me*! She looked like a waif on the stage! I, on the other hand, looked like a *star*!"

Sharpay and Ryan had both been asked to come back for the acting audition, but so had Anneclaire. Sharpay was still reeling from the injustice of this. "My costume alone deserved more applause!" she cried.

Ryan nodded vigorously, but then spoiled the moment. "And did you hear how people were cheering for her?" Sharpay shot him a venomous look. "They must have had too much coffee," he added quickly.

Meanwhile, Gabriella and Taylor were recapping their day. "I can't believe Chase got that question about nuclear fusion right! I had no idea what the answer was, did you?"

Taylor shook her head. "Nope. And I overheard Chase and Sinclair being interviewed for the behind-the-scenes segment. It turns out they've been tutored for two hours a day for the last year to prepare for this!"

"Really?" For a brief moment, Gabriella felt

sorry for them. "That doesn't sound like much fun."

"No, but it does sound like they're ready for the big time," Taylor said glumly. "Those dudes are so smart, they're scary."

Across the table, Troy and his teammates were going over their basketball game. "How did those guys spot our screens before we even set them? That's all I want to know," Troy said.

"Dude, I also want to know how they jumped so high, moved so fast, and managed to steal the ball every time I got my hands on it," Chad said.

"They don't even play as a team," Zeke agreed. "How did they get to be so good?"

Coach Bolton overheard this. "What are you guys talking about?"

"We got into a pickup game," Troy explained. "And it turns out the competition was a little tougher than we thought it would be."

His dad asked several more questions and, when he found out where they had played, he burst out laughing. "I don't believe it! You guys played in the Cage? That takes some guts."

The boys looked surprised. "Why?" Chad asked.

"It's famous, that's why! Some NBA stars got their start playing the Cage," Coach Bolton explained. "All the best players in the city play there, trying to make their mark. If you even held your own, that's something to be proud of."

Troy and Chad exchanged looks. "Well . . . I'm not sure we even did that," Troy said.

"Yeah, I guess we're not used to that style of play," Chad said.

"Maybe we should have gone someplace else if we wanted a game in New York," Zeke suggested. "Something more at our level—"

"Whoa, whoa!" Coach Bolton was shaking his head. "You got it all wrong."

"What do you mean?" Jason asked. "We were pulverized."

"Yeah, and that's great!" Their coach laughed at their confused expressions. "The only way to raise your game is to play against people who are better than you are. You shouldn't be upset if you're challenged or even if you lose, because that just means you had an opportunity to learn and improve."

"I hadn't thought about it like that," Troy said, already starting to feel better.

"Yeah, when we play against other high school teams, they probably won't seem as tough after what we went through in the Cage," Zeke said.

By now, everyone at the table was listening. Even Ms. Darbus was nodding in agreement.

"That's true," she said. She got a faraway look in her eye. "I well remember the time I was auditioning for the part of Evelyn Halsforth in *Starlight in Sandusky*. The girl I was up against had years more training, but that just made me dig deep into my soul! I discovered inner resources that I never knew I had, and I've been able to tap them ever since. That experience helped me grow as an actor, an artist, and a director!"

She sighed, enjoying the memory. Then she remembered where she was and gave Coach

Bolton an approving look. "That was very well put, Mr. Bolton—especially considering that your background has been focused on throwing a little ball around a gym."

The coach's expression wavered between surprise and irritation and finally settled on pleased. After all, he didn't get many compliments from Ms. Darbus, even backhanded ones!

The next morning, Troy, Chad, Zeke, and Jason went to a famous deli for breakfast because Zeke wanted to check out their handmade bagels. Then they stopped by a sporting-goods store to buy a basketball, found an empty court, and spent an hour practicing before heading to Chinatown for lunch.

"We seem to be playing better already," Troy commented, after they had all piled into a subway car to head downtown. "I've never seen Chad move so fast, and Jason, those three-pointers you hit were awesome!"

"I keep imagining Terence guarding me,"

Chad confessed. "That gets me moving every time!"

"And I kept thinking about how Bongo would steal the ball from me," Zeke said. "I think if I just do that little sidestep, I can stop him next time. At least, that's what I want to try."

"We only have a couple more days in New York, though," Jason said.

Troy nodded. "I think we should go back to the Cage tomorrow."

There was silence. "Tomorrow?" Chad said. "Really? 'Cause I know I'm moving faster, but I'm not sure I'm moving fast enough. At least, not yet."

"You heard what my dad said," Troy replied. "We gotta test ourselves to get better. If we know that's what we're doing, we won't care if we get stomped, as long as we learn something."

After a moment, Chad nodded. "Okay," he said. "I'm in."

"Me, too," Jason and Zeke said together.

Troy grinned. "Great. Oh, here's our stop. The kung pao chicken is on me!"

When Sharpay arrived at the theater for the acting audition, she looked around the room. "There aren't too many people left for the last audition," she said.

Ryan's eyes widened. "And more than two hundred people started out," he said in a hushed voice.

"Look at it this way," Ms. Darbus said. "Now you have even less competition."

"As if anyone here actually offered any kind of competition for me!" Sharpay sniffed.

"Remember, the acting audition will determine who gets cast," Ms. Darbus went on. "So I want to see you two get out there and dazzle everyone the way I know you can!"

Ryan nodded earnestly, but Sharpay wasn't listening. She had stayed up late studying the scene they were going to perform today, and she had been doing a lot of thinking. "Do you see Anneclaire anywhere?" she asked.

Ryan obediently scanned the room. "Nope. No supertalented diva on the horizon," he announced. "Oh, except you, of course."

"Hmm." Sharpay smiled to herself. "Well, let me know as soon as you see her, all right?"

Her brother looked at her, half-curious, half-fearful. "Why? What are you going to do?"

"Oh, let's just say that I have a little plan," Sharpay said.

"Ohhh." Ryan nodded in what he hoped was an intelligent way, even though he didn't know what she was talking about. All he knew was that when Sharpay had a plan, everyone else better get out of the way!

"All right, I'm going to match you kids up for these auditions," the director, Mr. Smith, announced. "Girls, you're going to be performing the cafeteria scene. Boys, you're going to do the locker-room scene. Okay! First up, Sharpay Evans and June Lawson—"

"Excuse me? Mr. Smith?" Sharpay raised her hand and ran up to the stage. Ryan and Ms. Darbus exchanged confused glances. What was Sharpay up to now?

Sharpay leaned over to whisper in Mr. Smith's ear. His eyebrows lifted in surprise, but he shrugged and nodded.

"Okay, people, change in plans," he said. "The first audition will be Sharpay Evans—performing with Anneclaire Littlefield."

Ryan's jaw dropped. He turned to Ms. Darbus and saw that her expression mirrored his own.

"Did Sharpay just say she wanted to audition with *Anneclaire*?" he asked.

Ms. Darbus nodded slowly, a small smile appearing on her face. "I think so," she said. "This should be interesting. . . ."

Sharpay and Anneclaire sat on folding chairs, facing each other on the stage and holding their scripts.

"'Well, the homecoming elections are over,'"

Anneclaire read. She gave Sharpay a slight smile and tilted her head just a bit. Even from the back of the auditorium, it was clear from Anneclaire's body language that her character was offering some sort of truce.

"'Yes, and I can't believe that I was elected homecoming queen instead of you!'" Sharpay's delivery was slightly exaggerated, but she quickly caught herself and delivered the next line with more feeling. "'After all, you did work awfully hard for it.'"

Anneclaire sighed. "'Maybe too hard,'" she said, with a slight catch in her throat. "'This whole experience has taught me a lot. About winning and losing . . . and friendship.'" A real tear rolled down her cheek. "'I'm sorry for all the things I did to you, like changing the appointments in your organizer so you missed the entry deadline, and putting food coloring in your shampoo!'"

"'Well, I would have done them to you if I'd thought of it!'" Sharpay added a glint of humor to the line, and heard people in the audience chuckle. Pleased, she went on, putting all the sincerity she could muster into the next line. "'I can't believe it took so long for us to realize that we're actually . . . pretty much alike.'"

She glanced up from the page. Anneclaire was looking right at her, totally in character. She gave Sharpay a little nod.

"'In fact, we're a *lot* alike,'" Sharpay went on, and the note of sudden realization in her voice wasn't all acting.

"'So what do you say?'" Anneclaire read her next line. "'Truce?'"

"'Truce,'" Sharpay said.

Anneclaire smiled at her. "Great. Now let's go have some fun!" she exclaimed.

Sharpay glanced down at her script, confused. That line wasn't in the play . . . Oh! She looked back up at Anneclaire and smiled. "Sounds good."

The director bounced onstage, calling out, "Very good work! Now, let's see who's up next. . . ."

CHAPTER EIGHT

"**H**ow's everybody doing? Are we all ready for the final round of *College Quizmaster*?" Bert, the producer, burst into the room, closely followed by Joe, who had his camera on his shoulder. They were already filming, even though it was only—Taylor yawned as she checked her watch—7:30 a.m.

"You bet we are," she said, trying to sound awake.

"And how do you guys feel, now that it's

down to just two teams?" Bert went on.

Chase and Sinclair gave each other a satisfied smirk. Winnie and Jan had been eliminated in the last round. "We're ready to roll on to victory," Chase said confidently.

"Not that these ladies aren't as bright as they are lovely," Sinclair added, with a nod at Taylor and Gabriella. "But we think we can beat them in the lightning round. We've been practicing that for six months."

Bert noticed how Taylor and Gabriella glared at Sinclair, annoyed by his condescending air. The producer rubbed his hands together gleefully at this sign of friction and decided to egg it on a bit. "Gabriella, you look like you have the eye of the tiger today! Are you ready to *take these guys out?*"

Gabriella opened her mouth to say something scathing, but remembered, just in time, that the camera was rolling. "Um, well, I'll certainly do my best," she said politely.

Bert rolled his eyes. "Taylor, what's your

game plan for beating Team Muskrat? They trounced Team Wildcat yesterday in the literature section. How are you going to come back from that?"

"They can always cross their fingers and hope no one brings up Faulkner," Chase whispered to Sinclair.

Taylor's eyes narrowed at the snide comment. "Since we outscored everyone in the science and math categories and were tied in the history category, I'm not worried about losing a few points in literature," she said sweetly.

Sinclair shook his head in mock sorrow. "I heard that you guys only decided to try out for *College Quizmaster* a few months ago. Chase and I, on the other hand, have been working toward this moment for two years! For the last six months, we spent two hours every day on drills, we read four newspapers a day to keep up with current events, and we hired a private tutor to simulate the actual game. We're better prepared than any other team in the country!"

"That *is* impressive." Bert turned to Gabriella, who was finding it harder and harder to smile. "What do you have to say to that?"

"Well, the final round always includes more pop culture questions, which I think will give us an advantage," she said evenly. "After all, life is about more than studying, right?"

Chase and Sinclair snickered at that. "Yeah," Chase said, "you just keep telling yourself that on your trip home . . . *losers.*"

"I am so mad, I could just . . . just spit!" Taylor fumed.

She and Gabriella had finally been left alone to prepare for the final round. They had fifteen minutes before they were going to be called onstage, and they were both trying their best to calm down. That wasn't easy, since Taylor was seething after Chase and Sinclair's remarks, and Gabriella was beginning to get the butterflies that she always had before going in front of an audience.

"How dare they talk to us like that?" Taylor went on.

"Don't you see, they wanted to make us mad?" Gabriella said. "That way, we won't be focused, we won't be on our game, and we'll lose. Not because they're any smarter than us, but because they got in our heads."

Taylor took a deep breath and released it slowly. "You're right," she said. "I know you're right. And that producer was really stirring it up, too, trying to freak all of us out."

Gabriella nodded. "I'm glad we didn't start talking trash about Chase and Sinclair on camera," she said, "even though they were doing that to us. I mean, come on, a quiz show isn't *that* important."

But Taylor was looking worried. "Those guys *have* spent a lot more time studying for this than we have," she pointed out. "They may be obnoxious when they brag about how smart they are, but they're not wrong."

"No," Gabriella said slowly. "Even when we

were in the Scholastic Decathlon, I felt like we had a decent chance of winning. But these guys are much tougher competition—"

"—and they've been studying for two years, and reading four papers a day, and they actually hired a *private tutor*!" Taylor was starting to hyperventilate. "How crazy is that? They just want the win more; that's all there is to it."

"No." Gabriella's voice was firm. "If they were that confident, they wouldn't have been playing head games with us. And remember what Coach Bolton said? Competing against someone who's good enough to challenge you only makes you better. And Taylor—" She gave her friend a wink. "—we're already pretty good."

Back in the Palace Theater, the level of excitement and anxiety had zoomed sky-high. The finalists had all gathered in the auditorium to hear the audition results. Who would be chosen for their Broadway debut? And who would be forced to watch as a member of the audience?

Everybody crossed their fingers and held their breath as they waited for Mr. Smith to announce the cast.

Out of the corner of her eye, Sharpay saw Anneclaire standing in the wings. Sharpay hesitated for a moment, then went over to her.

"Well, the auditions are finally over," she said. "I never thought I would say this to anyone, but I think you're *almost* as talented as I am."

"Funny, I was going to say the same thing to *you*," Anneclaire said. Then she added, "Maybe we're equally talented."

Sharpay thought this over for a second, then nodded. "That dance you choreographed was great," she admitted.

"The costume you pulled together was inspired," Anneclaire offered.

"Maybe we should stick together," Sharpay said. "After all, there aren't very many performers of our caliber out there!"

Anneclaire nodded. "Triple threats," she pointed out. "Acting, dancing, and . . ."

". . . singing," Sharpay chimed in. "Of course, I also produce," she added casually.

"Really? I've never done that," Anneclaire said.

"Oh?" Sharpay said, pleased. "Well, it's terribly draining to work with performers who aren't up to *our* standards, but I find it quite rewarding."

"That's exactly how I feel," Anneclaire said, "about all the shows I've directed."

Sharpay bit her lip, annoyed. Was this girl always going to try to one-up her? Then she remembered how her competition with Anneclaire had made her try harder at every stage of the auditions, and how acting with another talented performer had made her job so much easier. She decided that she could, just possibly, learn something here.

"I've always wanted to direct," she said. "I'd love to talk to you about that—"

But at that moment Mr. Smith stepped onto the stage, ready to announce his new cast. . . .

"This is a three-part question," the game show host said. "What is the largest continent on Earth? What theory states that the continents once formed one large land mass? And what was the name of that supercontinent?"

Gabriella's hand hit the buzzer. "Asia, the Continental Drift Theory, and, er—" She stopped, her mind blank.

"Pangaea," Taylor said quickly.

"Correct on all counts!" the host cried.

"Thanks," Gabriella whispered to Taylor.

"No problem." Taylor grinned at Chase and Sinclair, who were scowling. "No problem at all."

"Next question," the host said. "Also in three parts. What was the first city to reach a population of one million? When did that milestone occur? And what was the second city to hit that mark?"

Before the last word was out of his mouth, Chase had hit his button. "Ancient Rome, 5 BC, and London," he rattled off, adding smugly, "and London didn't reach a million people until 1800."

"Correct on all counts, no extra credit for the unasked-for information," the host said, frowning at Chase. He *really* hated show-offs. "Next question! I will read the opening lines from a series of classic books. Name the title and author of the book. Ready? 'There was no possibility of taking a walk that day—'"

Bzzz! "*Jane Eyre* by Charlotte Brontë," Sinclair said. He smirked at Taylor.

"Correct! 'Call me Ishmael—'"

Bzzz! "*Moby Dick* by Herman Melville," Taylor said. She smirked back.

"Correct! 'Christmas won't be Christmas without any presents—'"

Bzzz! "*Little Women* by Louisa May Alcott," Gabriella answered.

"Correct! 'Marley was dead, to begin with—'"

Bzzz! "*A Christmas Carol* by Charles Dickens," Chase said.

And so it went for question after question. Team Wildcat would pull ahead by a few points, only to be tied by Team Muskrat. Team Muskrat would have a winning streak, only to be overtaken by Team Wildcat. By the last minute of the round, everyone, including the normally debonair host, was sweating.

"I don't think we've ever had a closer contest on *College Quizmaster*," he said. "The score is tied 117 to 117. We have time for one last question. Here it is, the last question of the last round! The winners will each take home a $10,000 scholarship! The losers will receive *College Quizmaster* sweatshirts and caps! Are you ready?"

Chase and Sinclair gave each other smug looks. They looked relaxed and confident.

Gabriella and Taylor just nodded.

"Raising the game," Gabriella whispered to Taylor, who gave her a quick grin.

"Here it is, then, a three-part question: Michael Jordan is considered the best basketball player of all time. For the *College Quizmaster* championship—what team did he play for in the 1990s, how many championships did they win, and what other professional sport did he play?"

There was a long silence. Chase and Sinclair exchanged glances again, but this time they looked nervous and worried, rather than smug.

And Gabriella just smiled as she reached for her buzzer. . . .

"Hey, look who came back for another trouncing!" Reggie called out.

As Troy, Chad, Zeke, and Jason walked into the Cage, they were met by disbelieving smiles from the guys they had played before.

"I thought you boys might wait awhile before taking us on again," Terence said.

"Yeah, like another century," Reggie added. Max and Bongo elbowed each other, laughing.

Troy just smiled. "Hey, you guys have got some great moves," he said. "We just want to check them out again."

Terence looked at his friends and shrugged.

They shrugged back. "Okay, dawg," he said. "You're on."

Troy turned to his teammates. "Remember, let's stay calm and play our game," he said as they walked onto the small court.

"Right," Chad said, a determined gleam in his eye. "We gotta keep our heads in the game."

That was the last chance they had to say anything, because the action was just as fast as before. Bongo kept hitting three-pointers, Terence kept pulling off gravity-defying jump shots, Max kept stealing the ball, and Reggie kept getting rebounds. But there was one difference—the Wildcats were expecting these moves. They didn't get flustered or start trying to make wild shots. When the pace got too fast, Troy signaled his teammates and they slowed the play down, so their opponents had to match their pace.

After half an hour, they took a break. Sweating, the Wildcats huddled on the side of the court.

"They're still outscoring us two to one," Chad said, breathing hard.

"That's an improvement over last time," Jason pointed out. "That was more like a hundred to one!"

"And this feels better," Zeke added. "At least we're holding our own."

Troy nodded. "And now we can actually see some of their moves in time to react," he said. "Have you noticed that? Now, here's what I think we can work on next—"

By the end of the game, the Wildcats had actually managed to surprise their opponents a couple of times. Chad executed a fast drive to the basket, Troy faked out Reggie and tipped the ball in, and Zeke and Jason thwarted a couple of Terence's jump shots with intense defense.

As they walked off the court, Terence held out his hand to Troy. "Nice game today," he said. "You guys definitely got my respect."

"Thanks." Troy grinned as they shook hands.

"And thanks for the game. We learned a lot from you guys."

"Yeah," Reggie said. "I noticed that. Good thing you guys are heading home, or you'd be making trouble for us one of these days."

The Wildcats laughed.

"Yeah, right," Chad said. "You guys are awesome players. But I know one thing . . . I can't wait to pull some of these moves back home when basketball season starts again!"

CHAPTER NINE

On their last night in New York, all the Wildcats got dressed up in their best clothes and piled into cabs to go to the Palace Theater. They pushed their way through a throng of people in the lobby and found their seats. They chatted, read their programs, and waited with barely concealed impatience for the play to begin.

Finally, the lights dimmed, the audience hushed, the curtain rose . . .

. . . and the spotlight hit Sharpay and

105

Anneclaire standing at center stage. They were surrounded by two dozen other teenagers, including (in the back, at stage left) Ryan. The Wildcats cheered wildly, and Sharpay gave a slight smile in their direction. But then the music started and the first big musical number was underway.

For the next two hours, the cast of *Last Bell!* gave their one-night-only performance everything they had. By the time the curtain came down, the audience was on its feet, and everyone was dancing along to the last song.

The cast came out for their curtain calls, bowing and waving to friends in the audience. Ms. Darbus even ran up the aisle to the front of the stage and threw a bouquet of flowers to Sharpay.

"Brava!" she cried. "Brava—and bravo—to all of you!"

Zeke whipped out his camera and took as many shots of Sharpay as he could before the cast finally left the stage for good. "Just think," he said dreamily, "I was here to witness Sharpay's Broadway debut!"

"Yeah, it's a night that will go down in history," Chad said. "Or live in infamy." He paused, then added, "That's a tough one to call."

Backstage, Sharpay and Ryan hugged each other; then they hugged Anneclaire and anyone else within reach. When the rest of the Wildcats made their way to the dressing room, they got hugged as well. In the general excitement, Zeke even managed to get two hugs from Sharpay.

Before they headed off for dinner, Sharpay turned to Anneclaire. "Here's my e-mail address," she said. "Let me know when you're doing your next musical."

"Thanks," Anneclaire said. "I'll send you photos and all my reviews!" Then she caught herself and grinned. "I'd like to read *your* reviews, too, of course."

Sharpay grinned back.

* * *

"I can't believe it's almost time to go home," Gabriella said to Taylor. Everyone was milling around on the sidewalk outside the theater and trying to flag down a couple of cabs to take them back to their hotel.

"But we are going home with scholarships in our pockets," Taylor reminded her. She chuckled. "Not to mention the sweet memory of those boys' faces when you answered that last question! Girl, where did that come from?"

Gabriella grinned in Troy's direction. "I had a tutor, too," she teased. "Only he was teaching me all about basketball trivia."

"You're a good student," he teased back. "Being able to remember all that stuff about MJ and pulling it out right at the last buzzer . . . that is awesome!"

"I can't wait to hear about your return to the Cage," Gabriella said to Troy.

"Maybe we can take a walk tonight?" he suggested. "Just the two of us?"

"That sounds like a perfect end to our trip," she agreed.

Just then, two cabs screeched to a halt in front of them. "C'mon, let's go!" Coach Bolton called out.

"Wait a second!" Zeke whipped out his camera again. "Everybody get together in a group. . . ."

The Wildcats quickly threw their arms around each other and smiled as Zeke handed the camera to Ms. Darbus and ran to join them.

"Say *fromage!*" she called out.

But the Wildcats were already smiling. After all, they had faced their toughest competition ever and they had all come through—New York-style!

Something new is on the way!
Look for the next book in the Disney High
School Musical: Stories from East High series. . . .

HEART TO HEART

By Helen Perelman
Based on the Disney Channel Original Movie
"High School Musical", written by Peter Barsocchini

The East High auditorium was bustling as all the students filed in for the mandatory Monday morning assembly. When Gabriella Montez walked in, there was so much noise she could hardly hear her friend Taylor McKessie.

"What did you say?" Gabriella asked, leaning in closer to Taylor.

"I said," Taylor repeated, a bit louder this

time, "I can't believe we're missing chem lab for this." She gave her chemistry textbook a big hug. "I love chem lab."

Gabriella smiled. Most kids at East High were happy to have an assembly get-out-of-class-free card, but Taylor was different. As leader of the East High Scholastic Decathlon team, the girl was obsessed with school, especially science.

"Maybe it won't be the whole period," Gabriella said, trying to reassure her friend.

"Students, please come in and take a seat," Principal Matsui's voice boomed through the speakers. Onstage, the principal was gesturing for students to come in and sit down. He leaned in closer to the microphone that was perched on the podium. "We'd like to get started."

"Hey, Taylor! Hey, Gabriella!" Martha Cox called from the fifth row. Martha was on the Decathlon team and had saved some seats for them. She moved her bag and jacket, and motioned for them to join her.

"Thanks," Taylor said as she sat down.

"Hi," Gabriella said, though she couldn't help but be a bit distracted. Where was her friend Troy Bolton? Maybe he had thought to save her a seat, too? She didn't get to see him before home-room, and she was anxious to talk to him. They had talked on the phone the night before, but she always felt like she had so much to tell him.

"Good morning, students," Principal Matsui said.

The audience quieted down as everyone finally slid into their seats.

"It is my pleasure to welcome you to this special assembly about our participation in the United Heart Association Valentine's Day Challenge."

"Valentine's Day *is* a challenge!" someone from the crowd called out.

A roar of laughter came from the back of the auditorium.

Gabriella turned around. She thought it sounded like a comment Chad Danforth would make. He not only was a great basketball player, but he was also a jokester. In the back rows of the auditorium, she spotted Chad, laughing with his basketball-team buddies. Troy was sitting next to him. Just as she was about to turn back to face the stage, Troy caught her eye. Gabriella blushed and gave a small wave. Troy nodded and flashed her one of his dazzling smiles.

Chad's joke got the room buzzing, and Principal Matsui tried to quiet the crowd once again. He leaned closer to the microphone. "Heart to Heart is an annual fund-raiser and an excellent cause. You can all make a difference."

Gabriella turned to look back at Troy again. He was playing with the string from the hood on his sweatshirt. Gabriella smiled. Maybe this year Valentine's Day will be a little different, she thought as she settled back into her seat. As she turned her eyes back to the front of the auditorium, she wondered if Troy was thinking the same thing.

Principal Matsui was still speaking to the assembly. "This year, Sharpay Evans will be the captain of the event. She will let you know all the details. Please welcome her to the stage."

Sharpay walked up the steps to the stage as if she were at the Academy Awards® in a fancy ball gown. She took her time strutting up to the podium where Principal Matsui was standing. In her red velvet blazer and tailored white wool pants, she looked like a Valentine's Day art project.

"Hello, East High!" she greeted the crowd, turning on her charm full blast.

Ryan, Sharpay's brother and singing partner, and the drama club co-president, was sitting in the front row. He jumped up and gave a huge *whoop!* He then looked down the row at some of the other drama club members to follow his lead. A few clapped lightly.

"It is a pleasure to be here today," Sharpay said clearly and slowly. She was used to being onstage in front of the whole school. After all, she was the co-president of the drama club and the lead in most shows. Center stage was her home.

She looked down at the pink note cards that she had carefully prepared the night before. Being the captain of Heart to Heart was a huge responsibility and a big honor.

"Our goal this year is to raise the most money in the county for the United Heart Association. I have devised a plan to help us reach our goal." Sharpay looked up at her audience and gave them another huge smile. "Each school club will create a fund-raiser for the week of Valentine's Day. If we all work together, we can beat West High!"

Principal Matsui cleared his throat and stepped forward.

"I mean, we can raise a lot of money for the United Heart Association," Sharpay said. She couldn't help but mention West High. Their rival high school had won the challenge five years in a row. Now that Sharpay was the captain of the event, she was determined that East High would win.

"The drama club will be running the annual

flower delivery to homerooms on Valentine's Day. Forms will be available beginning on Monday." Sharpay paused and looked at her classmates. "Now remember, Wildcats, next Friday is Valentine's Day!"

"And not only that, we've got a game against South High!" Chad bellowed from the back. The students all cheered.

Sharpay smiled and held up her hand for quiet. "With the help of my drama club friends," Sharpay said, "we'd like to present, 'Flowers.' It's a little song that we came up with to express our feelings about the event."

On Sharpay's cue, Kelsi Nielsen, East High's most talented pianist and composer, entered from stage right pushing a piano. Ryan leaped up from his seat to join Sharpay on the stage. They had rehearsed this song and dance numerous times. Ryan loved the song. And clearly, he loved any chance to sing and dance.

Kelsi started to play the opening chords while Sharpay and Ryan moved the podium off to the side. They always liked to be in the middle of the stage for their routines.

Ryan got into position next to his sister and gave the audience a smile. Then he tilted his red cap forward over his eyes.

"How do you say you're special to a friend? What gives you the power?" Sharpay sang.

"A flower!" Ryan sang out in response.

"Yes," Sharpay bellowed in perfect pitch. *"Send a flower and make a donation to the United Heart. You'll be doing your part!"*

Gabriella turned around to look at Troy. He rolled his eyes and put his hands over his ears to block out the goofy song.

The performance had a big finish, with a short tap dance followed by a flip. Ryan and Sharpay held the last pose, waiting for applause. There were a few claps—mostly from the other drama club members seated in the first row. And, of course, Ms. Darbus, the drama teacher, always appreciated a good song-and-dance routine, so she joined in, clapping as loudly as she could.

But there were mostly groans from the rest of the audience.

"Oh, brother," Taylor whispered to Gabriella.

"Oh, brother and sister!" Gabriella said with a giggle.

"They need some new moves," mumbled Martha. She was very into hip-hop and was a great dancer herself.

Principal Matsui returned to the podium and took the microphone in his hands. "Thank you, Sharpay, Ryan, and Kelsi, for that interpretative routine," he said. "I hope that all of you will think about how you can contribute to this special school event."

The bell rang, and the students started to head out of the auditorium.

"Please report to your third-period class," the principal announced. "There will be a sign-up sheet outside the front office. I encourage every club to participate in this challenge. Thank you, East High!"

Taylor grabbed her backpack and stood up.

"Sharpay thinks that this is all about her. Well, this year, the Scholastic Decathlon team is going to raise the most money for the United Heart Association. I'm glad that we have a meeting today after school."

Gabriella raised an eyebrow. The Decathlon team was filled with some great people who knew lots of facts and figures. But what did they know about romance and Valentine's Day?

"Okay, guys," Taylor said, addressing the Decathlon team after school, "we can do this. We just need to think of one great idea."

The team was gathered in a classroom to discuss their fund-raiser for Heart to Heart. The buzz in the hallways all day was about the upcoming challenge.

"We're scientific people," Taylor told them. She looked at each one of her teammates seated at the table. "We can apply logic and brainpower to this problem. We will use proven scientific principles as our guide."

"Love is not scientific," Martha said.

The others nodded in agreement.

"We can come up with a good idea," Taylor said. "It's not like the only way to raise money is by delivering flowers." She got up and walked around the room.

"Well, giving flowers on Valentine's Day is an ancient tradition," offered Timothy Martin, a member of the team. "There's a long history of exchanging agricultural products as part of mating rituals."

"He has a point," Gabriella said. She didn't want to see Taylor upset, but she had to admit that Sharpay had secured the best idea for the Heart to Heart Challenge. They would have to think hard about creating another activity that would raise as much money.

"Maybe we should think outside the box," Martha said. She powered up her laptop. "Let's do some research on the history of Valentine's Day."

Soon the group was reviewing pages of

information Martha printed from the Internet. Gabriella stood back and looked at a list of facts about the romantic holiday. But she was distracted, thinking about what this Valentine's Day would mean for *her*. Should she buy Troy a Valentine's Day gift? she wondered. What should she get him?

Taylor walked over to the blackboard. "History isn't helping," she said. She took a piece of chalk in her hand. "Let's try to work this out mathematically. If Z equals love and Y equals Valentine's Day," she said writing the equation on the board, "then all we need to do is solve the equation for X. So clearly the problem is as simple as X equals Z minus Y!"

"The question is, what is X?" Martha said.

"And how much can we charge for it?" Taylor added.

"Is anyone else hungry?" Timothy moaned.

Gabriella smiled at Timothy. Then she said, "My mom always says the best way to a man's heart is through his stomach."

Taylor's face lit up. "That's it!" She rushed over to Gabriella and gave her a huge hug. "Oh, Gabriella," she gushed, "you are brilliant! You are absolutely brilliant!"

Gabriella smiled, but she was wondering what she said that had gotten Taylor so enthused.

COMING THIS FALL!

The must-have book for an
fan of *High School Music*

Includes lots o removable extr

Disney

HIGH SCHOOL MUSICAL ALL ACCES

TWINKLE TOWNE
A NEW MUSICAL

BASED ON THE HIT DISNEY CHANNEL ORIGI

WILDCATS

xperience the world of East High like never before with this comple
ind-the-scenes guide to *High School Musical* and *High School Musi*